C0-ALQ-907

nickelodeon

DORA the EXPLORER™

Take-Along Tunes

Storybook

Super Silly Fiesta

Story 2

Reader's Digest
Children's Books®

New York, New York ● Montréal, Québec ● Bath, United Kingdom

Play Song 1

One afternoon, Dora and Boots were being super silly together. Suddenly, Silly Mail Bird flew into Dora's room.

4

"Special delivery!" he said, looking through his mail bag full of silly stuff. He pulled out an invitation and handed it to his friends.

"Thanks!" said Boots. Dora opened it up.

"The Big Red Chicken is having a Super Silly Fiesta!" said Dora.

Play
Song
2

They asked Map how to get to the Fiesta.

"Go past the Mixed-up Farm, and over the Troll Bridge," said Map.

"*¡Vámonos!* Let's go!" said Dora.

Dora and Boots followed the path to Mixed-Up Farm. "Uh oh, I think these animals got all mixed up!" said Boots.

"*Quack!*" said the cow.

"*Moo!*" said the duck.

"*Neigh!*" said the chicken.

"*Bawk, bawk!*" said the horse.

WELCOME TO MIXED-UP FARM

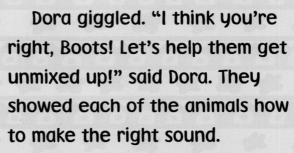

Dora giggled. "I think you're right, Boots! Let's help them get unmixed up!" said Dora. They showed each of the animals how to make the right sound.

"*Moo!*" said the cow.

"*Quack!*" said the duck.

"*Bawk, bawk!*" said the chicken.

"*Neigh!*" said the horse.

Play Song 4

At Troll Bridge, Dora and Boots saw their friend Benny. "I'm practicing juggling for the Fiesta!" he said. Just then, the Grumpy Old Troll popped out from under the bridge.

"You can't cross my bridge unless you can make me laugh," he grumbled.

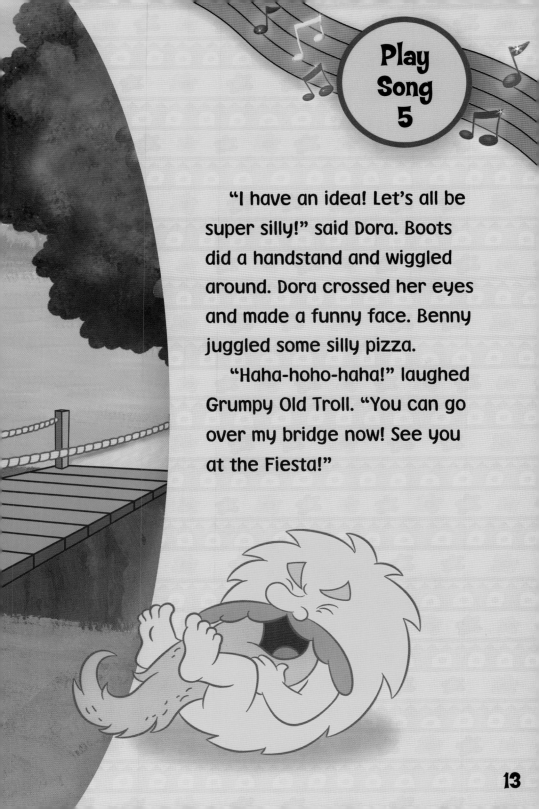

"I have an idea! Let's all be super silly!" said Dora. Boots did a handstand and wiggled around. Dora crossed her eyes and made a funny face. Benny juggled some silly pizza.

"Haha-hoho-haha!" laughed Grumpy Old Troll. "You can go over my bridge now! See you at the Fiesta!"

Dora and Boots made it to the Super Silly Fiesta. Big Red Chicken was very worried.

"Help, help! I lost my cake!" he cried.

"Hmmm...where did you have it last?" asked Dora.

15

Big Red Chicken thought for a moment. "I know! I put it on my head while I set the table. Then I put my hat on. Boy am I silly!" he said.

Big Red Chicken gave Dora a hug. "Thanks for helping me remember, Dora!"

Play Song 7

Big Red Chicken threw confetti in the air. "Now that we have the cake, we can start the party!" he announced.

"Hooray!" everyone cheered.

"Let's have a super silly time!" said Dora. The friends wore silly costumes, played silly games, and had the silliest Fiesta ever!

Song 1:
Someone's in the House with Dora

To the Tune of "Someone's in the Kitchen with Dinah"

Someone's in the house with Dora.
Someone's in the house, I know.
Someone's in the house with Dora
Playing on the piano.

Fee, fie, fiddle-e-i-o.
Fee, fie, fiddle-e-i-o-o-o-o.
Fee, fie, fiddle-e-i-o.
Playing on the piano.

Song 2:
Mixed-Up Animal Farm

To the tune of "Animal Fair"

I went to the mixed-up farm.
The cows and the ducks were alarmed.
The Big Red Chicken
By the side of the pen
Was hoofing toward the barn.

You should have seen the cow.
His beak made Boots say, "Wow!"
The ducks had snouts and swam all about,
At the mixed-up animal farm, at the mixed-up animal farm.

Song 3:
The More We Get Together

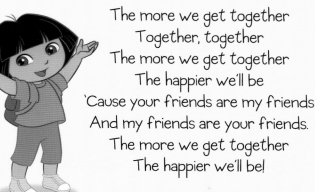

The more we get together
Together, together
The more we get together
The happier we'll be
'Cause your friends are my friends
And my friends are your friends.
The more we get together
The happier we'll be!

Song 4:
Does Your Beard Hang Low

Does your beard hang low?
Does it wobble to and fro?
Can you tie it in a knot?
Can you tie it in a bow?
Can you throw it over your shoulder
like a toy tin soldier?
Does your beard hang low?

Song 5:
Isa Dora Tico Benny Boots

To the tune of "John Jacob Jingleheimer Schmidt"

Map Dora Backpack Benny Boots,
Our friends are your friends, too.
Whenever we go out,
Exploring all about,
We sing Map Dora Backpack Benny Boots,
Dah dah dah dah, dah dah dah dah.

Song 6:
Super Silly Fiesta

To the tune of "Boom, Boom, Ain't It Great to be Crazy?"

A big red chicken threw a big party
With lots of food and the Fiesta Three,
The chicken slipped and fell off his bed,
"Whoops," he clucked, "there's a cake on my head!"

Boom, boom, ain't it great to be crazy?
Boom, boom, ain't it great to be crazy?
Giddy and foolish the whole day through,
Boom, boom, ain't it great to be crazy?

Song 7:
Ta Ra Ra Boom De-ay!

To the tune of Ta-Ra-Ra Boom-de-Ay!

Ta-ra-ra Fiesta day,
Ta-ra-ra Fiesta day!
Ta-ra-ra Fiesta day,
Ta-ra-ra Fiesta day!

Ta-ra-ra Fiesta day,
Ta-ra-ra Fiesta day!
Ta-ra-ra Fiesta day,
Ta-ra-ra Fiesta day!